Cat's Colours

* Jane Cabrera

for Julian &
Jerry~lee

a BIG
thank you
to Genevieve

Cat's Colours

Jane Cabrera

This book belongs to:

EGMONT CHILDREN'S BOOKS

Yellow

Purple

Orange

Blue

White

Red

Brown

Green

Pink

Black

Is it Green?
Green is the grass
where I like to walk.

Is it
Pink?
Pink are the petals
of my favourite
flowers.

Is it
Black?
Black is the night
when bats
swoop and soar.

Is it **Red?**
Red is the rug
where I snooze
by the fire.

Is it **Yellow?**

Yellow is the sand on the sunny beach.

Is it Purple?

Purple is the wool I tug with my claws.

Is it Brown?
Brown is the earth
where I dig my holes.

Is it Blue?
Blue is the sky where
I chase the birds.

Is it White?

White are the clouds floating in the sky.

Is it Orange?

Yes! Because...

Orange is the colour of Mummy.

First published in Great Britain 1997
by Heinemann Young Books and Mammoth
imprints of Egmont Children's Books Limited
a division of Egmont Holding Limited
239 Kensington High Street, London W8 6SA

Copyright © Jane Cabrera 1997
Jane Cabrera has asserted her moral rights

ISBN 0 7497 3120 6

A CIP catalogue record for this title
is available from the British Library

Printed in Hong Kong by Wing King Tong Co. Ltd.

5 7 9 10 8 6